Cold War Leaders

Wendy Conklin, M.A.

Publishing Credits

Historical Consultant
Shannon C. McCutchen

Editor
Torrey Maloof

Editorial Director
Emily R. Smith, M.A.Ed.

Editor-in-Chief
Sharon Coan, M.S.Ed.

Creative Director
Lee Aucoin

Illustration Manager
Timothy J. Bradley

Publisher
Rachelle Cracchiolo, M.S.Ed.

Teacher Created Materials
5301 Oceanus Drive
Huntington Beach, CA 92649-1030
http://www.tcmpub.com
ISBN 978-0-7439-0673-9

Table of Contents

A Cold World 4–5

Lenin in the Time of the Czars 6–7

Lenin's Great Ideas 8–9

Stalin and His Farmers 10–11

Moscow's Show Trials 12–13

Stalin's Constitution and Warnings 14–15

Khrushchev and His Speeches 16–17

Trouble with Cuba 18–19

A Showdown and a Race 20–21

The Beginning of Communism in China 22–23

Mao Tse-tung Rises to Power 24–25

Gorbachev, a New Kind of Communist 26–27

The End of a Cold War 28–29

Glossary 30

Index 31

Image Credits 32

A Cold World

Not too long ago, leaders in the world were very **cold** to each other. These leaders had some differences. Each side thought the other was wrong. Because of this, the Cold War developed.

Hot wars have soldiers, weapons, and battles. During a cold war, countries do not fight on battlefields. Instead, both sides store up weapons and threaten to use them. It is a contest to see who can be stronger. This is what happened in the world during the 1900s.

One side of the Cold War was fought by the West. This side included western nations like the United States, Great Britain, and France. On the other side were the Communists (KAHM-yuh-nistz). These leaders came from the Soviet Union, China, Korea, and Cuba.

The Cold War lasted from just after World War II to 1991. That's more than 40 long years! The leaders of these Cold War countries changed world history.

The United States and the Soviet Union built missiles that could travel from one country to another. These missiles could carry bombs.

The hammer and the sickle represented the Soviet Union during the Cold War.

Symbols

The hammer and sickle (SIH-kuhl) were on the Soviet Union's flag. The hammer symbolized workers. The sickle stood for the farmers.

Who Are the Soviets?

A soviet is a workers' council. These councils ran factories and local governments. They joined together and replaced the Russian empire. They used the name Soviet Union to show how they came together.

The West (blue) faced the East (red) in the Cold War.

Lenin in the Time of the Czars

Vladimir Lenin (VLAH-duh-mir LEH-nuhn) lived in Russia during the time of the **czars** (zars). A czar was like a king. He made all the laws and ran the country.

In 1905, Lenin did not like the way the czar ruled. So, he and others led a rebellion. But there were not enough rebels to overthrow the czar. The czar was very angry. He **exiled** (EKS-ziled) Lenin from the country.

Lenin had studied the ideas of a man named Karl Marx. Marx believed that people should work hard for their country. The country would then give everyone his or her fair share. **Peasants** would get to own land. Each person would get the same amount of food. This sounded like a good idea to Lenin.

Karl Marx

Lenin's Exile

Lenin spent time in Siberia, a very cold place in northeast Russia. From there, he went to Switzerland and Finland.

Marx's Mistake

Marx wanted to pay people whatever amount of money they needed. It did not matter how much they worked. They would get the same amount of money. He thought his idea would inspire people to work hard. Instead, it produced poor workers.

Vladimir Lenin speaks to a crowd in Moscow.

This poster shows the rulers of Russia. Nicholas II is at the bottom middle. He is the czar who exiled Lenin.

Lenin's Great Ideas

Lenin led a **political** group called the Bolsheviks (BOWL-shuh-vikz). The Bolsheviks believed that everyone should share the country's wealth. People should not have more than what they need. In the past, only a few rich people owned the land and everyone else worked it. Because of this, many peasants were very poor. The Bolsheviks hoped to change this.

Lenin wanted the workers and peasants to overthrow the czar. Then, they could set up a new system based on fairness. This new system was **communism** (KAHM-yuh-nih-zuhm). This was the opposite of **capitalism** (KAP-uh-tuhl-iz-uhm). Both communism and capitalism have to do with the **economy** (eh-KAH-nuh-mee). In a capitalist country,

These young Russian men followed the beliefs of Karl Marx. Lenin is seated behind the table.

Bolshevik leaders wanted to change life in Russia.

there is a big difference between the rich people and the poor people. Communists wanted to make sure that everyone had the same amount of money. This belief was based on Marx's ideas.

In 1917, Lenin heard about revolts in Russia. He went back to lead the people. He told them that if they wanted land and power, they had to take it. This was the Russian Revolution. The Bolsheviks led the workers to victory. The czar was overthrown. And, Lenin became the first leader of the new Soviet Union.

The Viks!

The Bolsheviks were a very **radical** group. They wanted big changes fast. There was another group called the Mensheviks (MEN-shuh-vikz). They were a **moderate** group. They felt it would take time for changes. The Mensheviks wanted to work with the government. On the other hand, the Bolsheviks wanted to set up a new government.

Women's Liberation

The Bolsheviks and Lenin made laws to support women. As Lenin said in 1921, "no trace is left of any inequality between men and women under the law . . . this is only the first step in the liberation of women." The laws were in place, but there was still a long way to go for equal treatment.

Stalin and His Farmers

Joseph Stalin led the Soviet Union from 1924–1953.

Bank Robber

When he was young, Stalin wanted to help the Bolsheviks. So he robbed banks and sent them the money.

Stalin and Women

During Stalin's rule, life for women got harder. The laws that had been set up by the Bolsheviks were failing. Women were forced to work, and they still had to take care of their homes and children.

Lenin died in 1924. A man named Joseph Stalin became the new leader of the Soviet Union. He had a five-year plan. He wanted to use Communist beliefs to make the country strong. His plan began with the farmers.

Farmers with land had to give it to the government and let others farm it. This idea caused problems right away. The rich farmers were angry. They did not want to lose their land. Some even had to share the equipment they had bought. Plus, the poor farmers did not want to work on other people's land. They wanted their own land. Farmers lost the passion to work.

Farmers began to lie about their crops. Then, the farmers started to hide their crops from the government. Stalin started to bribe poor, hungry people. He promised them food if they told officials where the crops were hidden.

Stalin tried to get the farmers to produce more food. He threatened and punished, but nothing seemed to work. Eventually, Stalin had to give in. He paid the farmers more money for their grain.

Young Communists dig up buried food in a cemetery. Wealthy farmers hid their grain rather than share it with others.

Women working on a farm in the Soviet Union.

Moscow's Show Trials

Many people criticized Stalin for his farming plan. In fact, even his wife spoke out against him at a party. Stalin did not like other people to question him. He could be very cruel to people who made him angry.

Often, people who disagreed with Stalin disappeared. It was assumed that they were killed. Stalin wanted to prove that he was not such a terrible man. So, he asked the **media** from other places to come see some trials. Today, these trials are called Moscow's show trials.

At these trials, prisoners marched in and confessed. After admitting their crimes, they asked to be punished. Most of the prisoners were shot by a firing squad or exiled out of the country. At first, the trials seemed fair. Then, they were studied more closely. It became clear that some of the prisoners had been forced to confess. Some of them were not guilty.

This poster of Stalin says, "We will achieve abundance!"

One of Joseph Stalin's show trials in the 1930s

Stalin's Paranoia

Stalin worried that people would try to **assassinate** (uh-SAS-suh-nate) him. He hired a bodyguard and stayed home much of the time. He also refused to tell anyone his schedule, not even his closest friends.

Stalin's Wives

Stalin's first wife died in 1907. He was very sad because of her death. Stalin married again. In 1932, Stalin and his second wife got into an argument at a party. She criticized him. After their fight, Stalin's wife died. She either killed herself or was murdered. Either way, people learned that they should not disagree with Stalin.

Stalin's Constitution and Warnings

In 1936, Stalin created a new set of laws. In it, he made many promises. Stalin promised that no one would be poor or without a job. All people over 23 could vote. They could have their own land if they wanted it. He even said that people would have freedom of speech. But, all these freedoms had to align with Stalin's wishes. So, people were not really free to say and do anything they wanted.

Stalin had always warned his people that capitalism was dangerous. But during World War II, Stalin needed help to fight the German Nazis. To win, he had to work with capitalist nations. The United States and Great Britain helped the Soviets win the war.

The friendship between these countries did not last long after the war ended. Both sides became distrustful of one another. They stopped talking and built weapons instead. A new kind of war started. It was called the Cold War. This war was between the East and the West.

Spreading Ideas

Stalin thought the West wanted to spread ideas about capitalism. The West thought Stalin wanted to spread ideas about communism. Both sides were right about the other.

The Iron Curtain

In March 1946, British leader Winston Churchill gave a speech. He said, "An iron curtain has descended across the continent." He meant that Stalin had taken over small nations in Eastern Europe and had made them Communist countries.

Winston Churchill

This Soviet poster promises joy and happiness to people who follow Stalin.

Stalin, President Roosevelt, and Winston Churchill met to discuss strategies during World War II.

Khrushchev and His Speeches

Joseph Stalin died in 1953. A few months later, a man named Nikita Khrushchev (nih-KEY-tah KROOSH-chev) took over. Khrushchev was a leader who liked to make speeches. One of his best-known speeches is his February 1956 "secret speech." He gave this speech to leaders of the Communist Party only. When they heard it, they could not believe their ears! In it, Khrushchev said Stalin had made Russia weak. Everyone thought of Stalin as a god. They could not believe Khrushchev had insulted him. Khrushchev wanted to change things, but he found this hard to do. However, after a short time, people started to agree with Khrushchev.

A few years later, Khrushchev spoke at the **United Nations**. During his speech, Khrushchev took off his shoe and banged it on the table. In Russian, he said that Russia would outlive the United States. Unfortunately, the **translator** said, "We will bury you!" Needless to say, dealings between Khrushchev and the West were not good after that.

Khrushchev pounds his fist against the podium.

A Russian peasant and a young boy work in a field.

Khrushchev waits his turn to speak at a United Nations General Assembly meeting.

Khrushchev the Poor Peasant

Khrushchev saw firsthand how badly Stalin treated his people. He grew up as a peasant farmer and knew how it felt to be poor.

No Disneyland for You!

When Khrushchev visited the United States, he traveled to many states. While he was in California, his family went to Disneyland. Khrushchev wanted to join them. The California police officers could not secure the park. So, he could not go. This made Khrushchev angry!

Gorbachev Likes What He Hears

After Khrushchev gave his secret speech, a young man named Mikhail Gorbachev heard about it. He secretly agreed with Khrushchev, but he did not say anything. At that point, it was dangerous to share your real feelings against Stalin.

Kennedy vs. Cuba

John F. Kennedy ran for president against Richard Nixon. Kennedy told Americans that he would be tough on the Soviet Union. He promised to make the United States military stronger. Kennedy wanted to end communism. He won the election and became president in 1961.

Kennedy first tried to end communism in Cuba. He failed with the Bay of Pigs invasion. This invasion made Khrushchev angry. Khrushchev soon placed nuclear missiles in Cuba. This caused the Cuban Missile Crisis in 1962.

Before he was assassinated in 1963, Kennedy signed the Partial Test Ban Treaty. This put an end to the testing of nuclear bombs on land. It was also the first step toward ending the Cold War.

Trouble with Cuba

Cuba is a Communist country. It is just 90 miles (145 km) south of Florida. In 1959, Cuba had a new leader named Fidel Castro (fee-DEL KAS-troh). Castro agreed with Marx and Lenin. He planned to set up a Communist government. Cubans soon learned that Castro was a **dictator**. This means that he controlled the country. He made all the decisions. This caused many people in the United States to worry. They did not like having a Communist dictator so close.

The United States planned a secret attack on Cuba. They hoped to throw out the Communist government there. This attack took place in April 1961 at the Bay of Pigs in Cuba. The plan failed and the United States had to admit they made a mistake.

Khrushchev wanted to protect Cuba. But, the Soviet Union was too far away from Cuba. So, Khrushchev planned to send **nuclear warheads** and **missiles** (MIS-suhlz) to Cuba. The United States president, John F. Kennedy, knew he had to do something.

President Kennedy displays the combat flag of the Cuban landing troops for the Bay of Pigs invasion.

Bay of Pigs invasion on April 15, 1961

A Showdown and a Race

A few nuclear missiles were already in Cuba. Khrushchev shipped some more missiles on large ships. Kennedy set up a **naval blockade** to stop the Soviet ships. The world watched as the Cuban Missile Crisis continued. Someone had to back down.

After 13 long days, both sides reached an agreement. Khrushchev agreed to remove the missiles. Kennedy promised he would leave Cuba alone.

Meanwhile, a space race was going on between the East and West. The Soviets sent the first **satellite** (SAT-uhl-lite) into space. It was called *Sputnik I*. They also sent the first man into space.

The United States wanted to be the first to land on the moon. In 1969, they were. Neil Armstrong and Buzz Aldrin walked on the moon. As he took his first step, Armstrong said, "That's one small step for [a] man; one giant leap for mankind."

In 1961, this Soviet rocket took Yuri Gagarin (YUR-ee guh-GAWR-uhn) into space. He was the first human to go into space.

Apollo II lifts off carrying Neil Armstrong, Michael Collins, and Buzz Aldrin.

Aldrin climbs down a ladder to walk on the moon.

Johnson in Vietnam

Lyndon B. Johnson became president after John F. Kennedy was assassinated. While president, Kennedy had sent U.S. troops and military advisors to South Vietnam. South Vietnam was trying to keep its independence from North Vietnam. North Vietnam was a Communist country. Its leader was a man named Ho Chi Minh (HOH-chee-MIN).

Johnson sent a large number of U.S. troops to South Vietnam to help fight against the Communists. But it did not work.

In 1967, Johnson wrote a letter to Ho. Johnson wanted to end the long conflict. He wanted North Vietnam to stop invading South Vietnam. Ho wanted the United States to stop helping South Vietnam. The two leaders could not agree on a solution. The conflict continued until 1975.

What's in a Name?

Mao Tse-tung is the same person as Mao Zedong. His family name is Mao. That is the same as a last name. Tse-tung or Zedong are both ways of spelling his Chinese name. They are both pronounced the same way.

Learning at the Library

While a young man, Mao was offered a library job at a university. He accepted it even though it paid poorly. He knew he could learn from the smart men who worked at the university. This was probably Mao's first introduction to Marxism.

A painting of the young Mao Tse-tung

The Beginning of Communism in China

In the Far East, communism was beginning to take hold, too. A man named Mao Tse-tung (MAU zuh-DUNG) took an interest in Karl Marx's ideas. Mao was born in the country and knew many peasants. This background gave him a bright idea. Maybe the peasants could bring communism to China? No one had ever thought much of the peasants. Most people believed they were only good for working. It became Mao's mission to teach the peasants these ideas.

For hundreds of years, **emperors** had ruled China. In 1911, the Chinese got rid of their last emperor. The people did not want emperors anymore. They wondered who would lead them next.

A **republic** was set up, but it did not work very well. The leader still wanted to be an emperor. The people did not want that. The Chinese people knew they needed a new kind of leader.

Mao gives a speech to a group of Chinese people.

Japanese soldiers invaded China in the 1930s.

Mao Tse-tung Rises to Power

A fight to take over China began between two groups. One was the Communists and the other was the Nationalists (NASH-uh-nuhl-istz). The Communists looked to Mao Tse-tung as their leader. They knew he wanted the peasants and poor to have the land. The Nationalists looked to the wealthy for support. The rich people were the landowners. For a while, the two groups tried to work together. But their differences proved to be too great.

World War II brought some big problems to China, though. The Japanese attacked China and wanted to take over. The Communists and Nationalists knew they had to work together. They joined with the **Allied forces** and won the war.

After the war, these two groups went back to fighting with each other. Peasants rose up and fought for Mao. The Communists won in 1949, and Mao became their leader. This was the beginning of the Communist People's Republic of China.

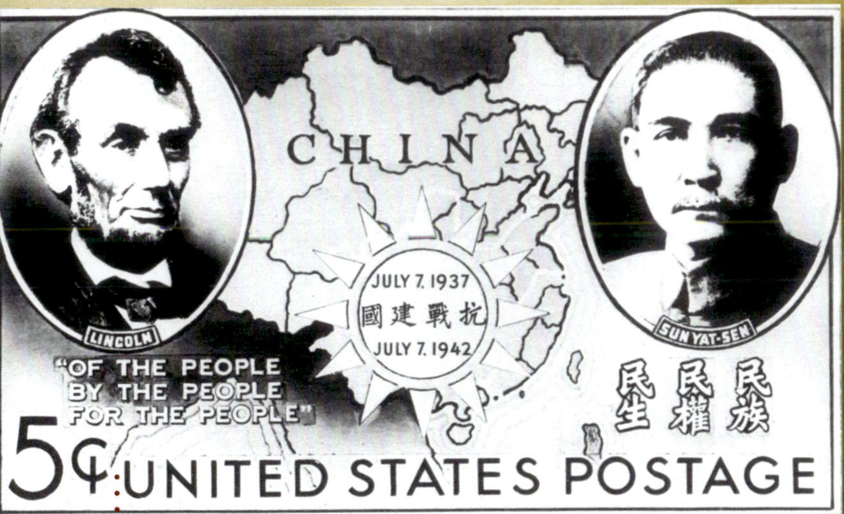

The United States and China were allies in World War II. When China became a Communist country, the United States did not support its former ally.

Nixon Goes to China

When Richard Nixon became president in 1969, he wanted to improve America's relationships with the Soviet Union and China. He also wanted to end the war in Vietnam. Nixon traveled to the Soviet Union to meet with its leaders. The Soviet Union and America soon agreed to limit their nuclear weapons. It was a step in the right direction.

Nixon then helped China become part of the United Nations. In 1972, Nixon shocked the world when he visited China. Nixon met with Mao Tse-tung. The meeting went well.

Nixon also tried to end the conflict in Vietnam. He ordered lots of bombs to be dropped in Vietnam. This made some Americans angry. In March 1973, Nixon ordered all the U.S. troops to leave Vietnam.

Gorbachev, a New Kind of Communist

In 1985, a new kind of Communist leader came to power in the Soviet Union. His name was Mikhail Gorbachev (mick-HAIL GORE-buh-chof). He wanted businesses to compete. He said that the press should have freedom of speech. These were new ideas for a Communist

Reagan Builds U.S. Strength

Ronald Reagan was a sports announcer and movie actor. Then, he became governor of California. And in 1981, he became president of the United States.

Reagan believed he could end the Cold War by gaining "peace through strength." He had the government spend lots of money on building more weapons. The Soviet Union heard about this, and they did the same thing. The United States started to build weapons that would stop nuclear missiles in the air. This way the missiles would not reach America. Reagan thought this would end the Cold War. But building these weapons was hard, and no one knew if they would work.

Gorbachev realized that his country spent too much money on weapons. He knew the Cold War needed to end before something terrible happened. In 1987, he met with Reagan and the two leaders worked together to help end the long Cold War.

country. Many Soviet leaders did not like him because of this. They were afraid to let people have freedoms. They wondered if these ideas could work in the Soviet Union.

At that time, Ronald Reagan was the United States president. Both sides had spent too much money on weapons. And, many people in the world lived in fear. People believed there could be a nuclear war at any time.

Gorbachev and Reagan decided to meet. They knew the **arms race** had to come to an end for the sake of future generations. Over time they agreed to reduce their weapons. It was a victory for the entire world. The Cold War was almost over.

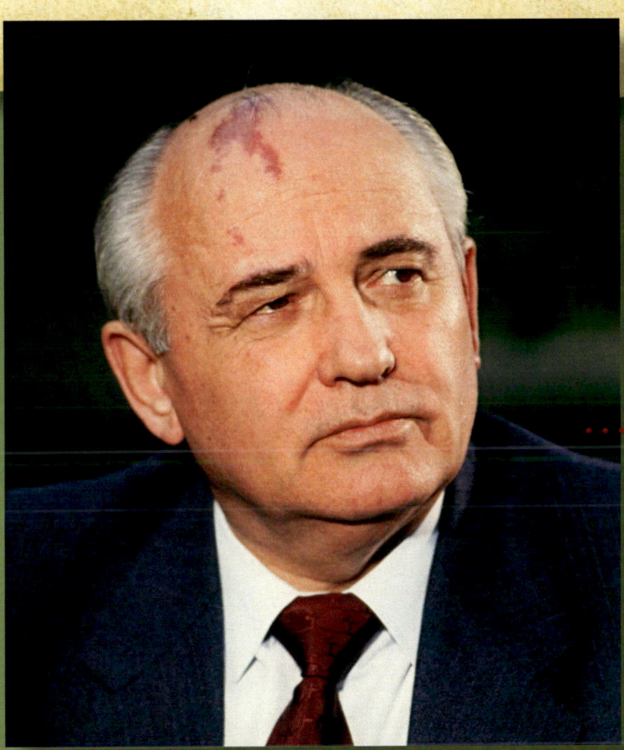

Gorbachev has an unusual birthmark on his forehead. Some Soviets thought it was a sign that he would rule for seven years. They were almost right; he ruled for six years.

President Reagan and Gorbachev discuss putting an end to the arms race between the Soviet Union and the United States.

The End of a Cold War

The Cold War lasted for more than 40 years. It was a war fought because of differences. The Soviets believed a person should work hard for his government. This hard work would make them stronger than the capitalistic nations. The United States felt people should choose how to spend their lives.

The Communist leaders changed their countries. They wanted to make communism work better. In the end, the changes brought **democracy** to some of these nations. People wanted to own land and make a profit. They needed personal reasons to work hard. People did not like their governments telling them what to do.

Today, China remains a Communist country. This is Shanghai, China.

Cuba is still a Communist country. This picture shows Havana, Cuba.

There are still Communist nations today. There are nuclear weapons today, too. The world is still learning how to deal with its differences. Maybe some of the lessons learned during the Cold War will help leaders today.

Bush and the End

George H.W. Bush was elected president in 1988. Communism was beginning to fail in Europe. Bush met with Soviet leader Gorbachev in December 1989. These meetings were called the Malta Summit. At the end of the meetings, the two leaders declared the Cold War officially over. Both sides agreed to reduce their weapons and armies.

Bush believed everlasting peace had been achieved between the East and West. Gorbachev promised Bush he would never start a nuclear war with the United States. In 1991, both Bush and Gorbachev signed the Strategic Arms Reduction Treaty. The two countries started to get rid of many of their nuclear weapons. People began to feel at ease again knowing the Cold War was over.

Glossary

Allied forces—Great Britain, France, the Soviet Union, and the United States

arms race—a time when countries each try to produce the strongest weapons

assassinate—to murder by surprise attack; usually a prominent person for political reasons

capitalism—an economic idea that lets people control their own businesses

cold—a lack of compassion or friendliness

communism—an economic policy where the government distributes all land and goods equally to the people

czars—rulers or emperors of Russia long ago

democracy—a government system where the people elect the leaders

dictator—a ruler who has total control

economy—the way a nation runs its industry, trade, and finance

emperors—rulers of a country or nation

exiled—forced absence from a homeland

media—newspaper, television, or radio

missiles—objects that can be projected long distances

moderate—in the middle; not extreme

naval blockade—to block ships with other ships at sea

nuclear warheads—sections of missiles with the explosives

peasants—farmers who work in European countries

political—concerned with government or politics

radical—extreme

republic—a nation where the power rests with the people

satellite—an object in space that orbits a larger object; human-made objects put into space to orbit Earth

translator—someone who turns one language into another language

United Nations—a group of countries who have promised to promote peace in the world

Index

Aldrin, Buzz, 20–21
America, 25–26
Apollo 11, 21
Armstrong, Neil, 20–21
Bay of Pigs, 18–19
Bolsheviks, 8–10
Bush, George H. W., 29
California, 17, 26
capitalism, 8, 14
Castro, Fidel, 18
China, 4, 23–25, 28
Churchill, Winston, 14–15
Collins, Michael, 21
communism, 8, 14, 18, 23, 28–29
Communist(s), 4, 9–11, 14, 16, 18, 21, 24–26, 28–29
Cuba, 4, 18–20, 29
Cuban Missile Crisis, 18, 20
Disneyland, 17
Gagarin, Yuri, 20
Gorbachev, Mikhail, 17, 26–27, 29
Great Britain, 4, 14
Eastern Europe, 14
Europe, 29
Finland, 6
Florida, 18
France, 4
Ho Chi Minh, 21
iron curtain, 14
Johnson, Lyndon B., 21
Kennedy, John F., 18–21
Khrushchev, Nikita, 16–18, 20
Korea, 4
Lenin, Vladimir, 6–10, 18
Malta Summit, 29
Mao Tse-tung (Zedong), 22–25
Marx, Karl, 6, 8–9, 18, 23
Marxism, 22
Mensheviks, 9
Moscow, 7, 12
Nationalists, 24–25
Nazis, 14
Nicholas II, 7
Nixon, Richard, 18, 25
North Vietnam, 21
nuclear bombs, 18
Partial Test Ban Treaty, 18
People's Republic of China, 25
Reagan, Ronald, 26–27
Roosevelt, Franklin, 15
Russia, 6–7, 9, 16
Russian empire, 5
Russian Revolution, 9
Siberia, 6
South Vietnam, 21
Soviet Union, 4–5, 9–11, 18, 25–27
Sputnik I, 20
Stalin, Joseph, 10, 12–17
Strategic Arms Reduction Treaty, 29
Switzerland, 6
United Nations, 16–17
United States, 4, 14, 16–18, 20–21, 25–29
Vietnam, 25
World War II, 4, 14–15, 25

Image Credits

cover Peter Turnley/Corbis; p.1 Peter Turnley/Corbis; p.4 Dmitry Nikolaev/Shutterstock, Inc.; p.5 (top) Alexander Pypin/Shutterstock, Inc.; p.5 (bottom) Chen Ping Hung/Shutterstock, Inc.; p.6 The Library of Congress; p.7 (top) Photos.com; p.7 (bottom) The Library of Congress; p.8 The Granger Collection, New York; pp.8–9 The Library of Congress; p.10 The Library of Congress; p.11 (top) Bettmann/Corbis; p.11 (bottom) The Library of Congress; p.12 The Granger Collection, New York; p.13 Bettmann/Corbis; p.14 The Library of Congress; p.15 (top) Thomas Johnson/Sygma/Corbis; p.15 (bottom) The Library of Congress; p.16 Bettmann/Corbis; p.17 (top) The Library of Congress; p.17 (bottom) The Library of Congress; p.18 The Library of Congress; p.19 (top) Corbis; p.19 (bottom) Bettmann/Corbis; p.20 Bettmann/Corbis; p.21 (top) National Aeronautics and Space Administration; p.21 (bottom) National Aeronautics and Space Administration; p.22 The Granger Collection, New York; p.23 The Granger Collection, New York; p.24 The Granger Collection, New York; p.25 The Granger Collection, New York; p.26 Bettmann/Corbis; p.27 Peter Turnley/Corbis; p.28 Amy Nichole Harris/Shutterstock, Inc.; p.29 (left) Bruno Medley/ Shutterstock, Inc.; p.29 (right) The Library of Congress